For my daughter, Sarah, and for the one who taught me
everything about being a mom—my mom, Sally
—JCN

For Neina, who is always bright
—SS

 little bee books

An imprint of Bonnier Publishing USA
251 Park Avenue South, New York, NY 10010
Text copyright © 2018 by Judy Carey Nevin
Illustrations copyright © 2018 by Stephanie Six
Manufactured in China HH 0118
First Edition 10 9 8 7 6 5 4 3 2 1
ISBN 978-1-4998-0528-4
littlebeebooks.com
bonnierpublishingusa.com
Library of Congress Cataloging-in-Publication Data
Names: Nevin, Judy Carey, author. | Six, Stephanie, illustrator.
Title: What mommies like / by Judy Carey Nevin; illustrated by Stephanie Six.
Description: First edition. | New York, NY: Little Bee Books, [2018]
Summary: Illustrations and simple text reveal what mothers like through
how they play with their babies. | Identifiers: LCCN 2017004958
Subjects: | CYAC: Mothers—Fiction. | Babies—Fiction. | Parent and
child—Fiction. | Classification: LCC PZ7.1.N485 Wl 2018 | DDC [E]—dc23
LC record available at https://lccn.loc.gov/2017004958

What Mommies Like

by Judy Carey Nevin   illustrated by Stephanie Six

little bee books

Mommies like
big hugs.

Mommies like kisses.

Mommies like "Good morning to you!"

Mommies like
field trips.

Mommies like bike rides.

Mommies like the library, too.

Mommies like stomping.

Mommies like clapping.

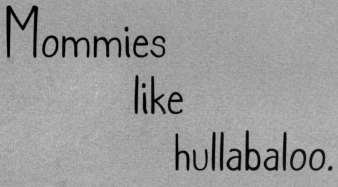

Mommies
like
hullabaloo.

Mommies like singing.

Mommies like drumming.

Mommies like
playing kazoo.

Mommies like reading.

Mommies like listening.

Mommies like bookmarks, too.

Mommies like bath time.

Mommies like cuddles.

And most of all...

Mommies like "I love you!"